Presented By
The Friends of
Nonesuch Books & Cards

The Best Bottom

Le Plus Joli Derrière © Mijade Publications—Belgium
Text © 2002 Brigitte Minne
Illustration © 2002 Marjolein Pottie

A publication of
Milk and Cookies Press, a division of ibooks, inc.

Distributed by Simon & Schuster, Inc.
1230 Avenue of the Americas, New York, NY 10020

This book is a work of fiction.
Any resemblance to actual events or locales or persons, living or dead, is entirely coincidental.

ibooks, inc.
24 West 25th Street, 11th floor, New York, NY 10010

The ibooks, inc. World Wide Web Site address is:
http://www.ibooks.net

ISBN: 0-689-03595-0
First ibooks, inc. printing: September 2004
10 9 8 7 6 5 4 3 2

Editor – Dinah Dunn

Library of Congress Cataloging-in-Publication Data available

Manufactured in the U.S.A.

The Best Bottom

Brigitte Minne

Marjolein Pottie

Frog was taking a nap on a lily pad.

She awoke, stretched and looked at the farm
that surrounded her pond. Frog knew everyone
at the farm and everyone at the farm knew her.
When one of her animal friends walked by the
pond, they often stopped to talk.

That day, Frog decided to venture out of the pond. She hopped over to the farmyard where Peacock was strutting around. As Frog drew close, Peacock spread his tail feathers. "Have I shown you my beautiful tail?" he asked. "Isn't it the loveliest you've ever seen?"

Before Frog could answer, Pig lifted his snout out of a pile of manure and grunted, "It's pretty but my tail is wonderful—it's pink and curls like a corkscrew!"

Donkey overheard Pig and laughed.
"A tail like that won't end well," he said. "Better to have a tail like mine. It is much less appetizing and much more elegant."

"Elegant?" barked Dog. "That mangy thing? There is no better tail than mine. What style! What shine! Even a fox would envy it!"

Soon all of the animals on the farm
were looking at their own bottoms,
each one sure that they had the best tail.
Cat was admiring the stripes on her long,
slender one. Horse, who had just been
groomed, was swinging his tail back
and forth. Rabbit admired his soft pompom.
Goat flicked her white tail from side to side.
Sheep ruffled his ringlets and Rooster
fluttered his beautiful tuft.
But who had the nicest tail?
Everyone, including Frog, wanted to know.

Cow, who was very wise, had an idea. "Let's have a contest!" she said. "My sisters and I could be the judges." Everyone agreed that a contest was a splendid idea.

They began to prepare for the judging. Rabbit fluffed the leaves from his pompom. Dog smoothed his tail with his teeth. Pig washed his corkscrew in the pond. Everybody was busy!

Frog also wanted to enter the contest, but she really
didn't have a tail—just a little green hump at the end
of her back! She was so sad to be missing out on all
of the fun.

But the other animals weren't having fun at all.
They had begun arguing among themselves
because they all wanted to win so badly.

Frog asked Cow to sign her up for the contest.
Cow shook her head sadly and said, "You know you have
the least chance of winning."
Frog shrugged her shoulders and replied, "I know but I
thought it could be fun."
"Okay, then," Cow said and added Frog to the list.

The other animals had a good laugh when
they heard about Frog.
"We like you Frog!" laughed Donkey, "But come on,
you don't even have a tail!"
Frog just smiled and started picking flowers.
"Look," said Pig, "she's making a bouquet for the
winner. How sweet!"

When the time for the contest finally arrived, the animals were still arguing about which one had the best bottom.

"My tail's going to win," bragged Peacock.

"Don't be too sure," Dog barked back.

"Mine is the cutest," said Rabbit.

"But I have a corkscrew," grunted Pig.

"Too bad it's so pink," brayed Donkey. "I hate pink!"

"Well lucky for me my tail is black as night," Horse said.

"More like black as the bottom of a shoe," Rooster crowed.

"The bottom of a shoe! I don't have to take that from a stupid rooster!" Horse neighed.

"That's right," added Donkey.

"Mind your own business, Donkey," bleated Sheep.

"Yeah," said Goat. "Mind your own business!"

"Who asked you?" hissed Cat to Goat.

"What a surprise—a cat being rude," sneered Goat.

"Not as rude as my claws," warned Cat.

At that moment, Goat lifted her hooves and tried to kick Cat. But Cat ducked and Rabbit got kicked instead. Rabbit flew into Donkey, who backed up and stepped on Rooster's foot. Rooster jumped on Donkey's back and started pecking at his ears.

Soon all of the animals were fighting. Fur and feathers were flying everywhere! In the middle of the fight, Cow called the animals to the stage to begin the contest.

The animals glumly made their way
across the stage, dragging their tattered tails
behind them. When Frog was called to the stage, she was wearing
a bouquet of beautiful flowers on her tail and it looked great!
Cow and her sisters applauded wildly at her creativity.
"Frog is the winner!" they cried.

The other animals, ashamed at their behavior, gladly crowned Frog the winner.

Hooray for Frog!